I0829662

How to catch a Thot
JEWLEYOUSE MERANCES

ISBN: 978-0-692-07681-1

Contents

Thot Rules

- ❖ Never turn a ho into a housewife.
- ❖ Don't you ever—and I mean, ever—kiss mouth-to-mouth!
- ❖ Repeat rule 1.
- ❖ Never exchange social media contacts.
- ❖ Never go out in public.
- ❖ Always wear a condom (maybe two to be on the safe side).
- ❖ Never have sex more than one or two times.
- ❖ Never let them know your real name.
- ❖ No holding hands, no cuddling, and no romancing.
- ❖ No dope dicking.
- ❖ Always be prepared with liquor or weed.
- ❖ Check to see if they have dirty feet. If so, don't smash!
- ❖ No spending time on holidays.
- ❖ No exchanging gifts (such as birthday, Christmas, etc.).
- ❖ Refer to rule 1.
- ❖ Never lend money out or ask for them to give you money.
- ❖ Never take pictures together.
- ❖ Always make the decisions for both of y'all.
- ❖ Never spend too much time with her.

Fuckboy Rules

- ❖ Never let him know where you live.

- ❖ Don't ever give him money.

- ❖ Don't give him any pussy after the first month.

- ❖ Don't vent to him about your problems.

- ❖ Don't let him know who your exes are.

- ❖ Don't agree to meet his parents.

- ❖ Don't make him meet any of your friends.

- ❖ Always act like you're broke.

- ❖ Never show feelings for him.

- ❖ Don't let him drive your car.

- ❖ Don't answer your phone after 12:00 a.m.

- ❖ Always use a condom.

Introduction

Thot is a denigrative slang term, originally defined as an acronym of "that ho over there," but is now generally used as a synonym for "ho" or "slut," epecially in the context of trap music or modern rap. The exact origin of "thot" is unknown. However, the word was first defined on Urban Dictionary on December 5, 2012, and it has since been independently defined 127 times. The magazine Complex claims that it originated in the Chicago drill-music community and was first popularized by the local rapper Katie Got Bandz in her song "Ridin' Round and We Drillin'," released on March 12, 2012. On April 30, 2012, another Chicago rapper named TKO released a single called "I Need a Thot." Also according to Complex, a man named Duan Gaines claimed to have first heard the term on set for a video shoot with Chief Keef. He then began using it on social media, popularizing the term.

CHAPTER 1

What Is a Thot?

A word itself came to be. As you may have already guessed, the word is frequently used in an unpleasant and problematic way. Rappers and hip hop artists use it as a derogatory term to describe women to whom they intend to pay no mind and whom they dismiss entirely. Why the dismissal? Because, as those who use the term see it, "They're just hos," and their worth is apparently wholly tied in with their sexuality and sexual prowess. This is presumably why the rapper Shamis says that "you can't make a thot a wife." Thots, by definition, aren't considered particularly desirable because they sleep around and will inevitably cheat on you, because a sexual woman is apparently incapable of being faithful; it is presumed that thots have no other qualities besides being hos. The term is popularly integrated into several hashtags, including #thotsbelike, which is popular on Instagram, and #youknowyouathot, which is popular on Twitter. On Instagram, the tag #thotsbelike has over 91,000 posts as of June 2015. The term "thot" returned over 91,000 results on Vine in the same period.

Criticism

The criticisms of the word "thot" are similar to that of its synonyms. Writers have called the term misogynistic, but some have identified it as also being a classist slur, similar to the basic "bitch" and "ratchet." These two terms identify a woman who is not only sexually open but is also interested in using her sexuality to receive inexpensive goods. To follow this guide, you will have to throw everything you know about picking up women out the window. If you need a book that teaches you how to find your soul mate or a potential girlfriend, this is not that book. This book will build the self-confidence you need to get any thot you want. Understanding thots is an easy task; you just have to know what they want and where to find them. Secondly, don't ever think pussy is free. I find it puzzling that some guys believe it is. The only people who think like that are probably people who do not get any pussy: the "forty-year-old virgin" type of person, or "incels." No matter what, you will have to spend money, such as funds for gas to find or money to pick up the thots (women). You may also spend money on drinks, so don't think you aren't about to come out of your pocket. I will teach you how to get a thot in the most natural way without hurting your pocket. The process is natural; it is all about knowing the right time and location. After reading this book, you will be well informed about what to look for when talking to a thot. So quit wasting your time at bars and clubs; remember that time is money, money is time, and your time is valuable. Getting pussy for tonight should be your second priority; your first priority should be to avoid spending as much money as you can while trying to complete this task. This could be expensive if you are a SIMP, but this book will arm you with the necessary tools for catching a thot. This book will help you avoid falling into that "super-save-a-hoe" category.

Let's get to work. Have you ever thought, "Damn, all I want is a thot tonight? I am not trying to cuff her up, I'm not trying to marry her; we're just going to fuck, and if it is good, I just might remember her name." First, you must handle this situation like it's a job because it is. All you need to do is go back to your rat trap. If this thot wants to drink, do you have liquor in your home for her? What if she is more of a smoker? Do you have weed? If she is hungry, do you have any food in your fridge? I'm not talking about warming up packages of ramen noodles either. I ask these questions because I know you do not want to waste money feeding her. Ask yourself these questions because hospitality is key. You should already have both white and dark liquor in your place. One more thing: never give this thot an option to choose what the hell she wants to drink. If you did, you just fucked yourself, player. This thot is drinking whatever the fuck you're buying.

I am going to start you off slowly. Abudget needs to be established when dealing with a thot. Your budget should between zero and twenty dollars—I repeat, no more than twenty dollars. Now that we have established a budget, let's talk about how you are going to make this budget work in both of your favors. Now, with twenty dollars, you go straight to the weed man and buy a bag; make sure it's a nice-sized one. Some women who smoke might want some loud or kush, or even some white. Kush is just a higher grade of weed, but it might cost you ten bucks. Personally, I think you should go with the "reggie." Remember, family, she should not have a say-so on the shit you're buying. You should also follow up with your neighborhood weed man to restock on everything you need because running out to the store to get something could become annoying and tedious. So my advice is to buy all you feel you need. After buying what you need, I believe you are ready to hit the streets and pick up some thots.

Every city is different, and every neighborhood is not the same, but all thots are. You just have to know what to look for when it comes to catching a thot. Generally speaking, 85 percent of thots like to get tattoos on their lower backs. We all know this to be true. And we used to call that the "tramp stamp" is presently the "thot stamp." But both stamps carry the same weight. If she has more than one baby daddy tatted on her body, yup, you guessed it, she is a thot. Every time you hit the club on different occasions—and it just so happens that these same women are in there—yup, you guessed it, they are club thots. If she is at the bar every time and you see her talking to different dudes, and they are buying her drinks, either she is an escort or a bar thot. These are just some of the ways to recognize particular thots, but there are many different kinds of thots to look for besides the ones I just mentioned.

At this point you have everything you need, so let's go thot fishing. You should understand that time is against you in a situation like this. You have from 7:30 p.m. to midnight to make your rounds in finding a thot. The timing is vital because the rush hour has died down. So you don't have to be worried about traffic and have a clear view of what you're looking for.

CHAPTER 2

Street Thot

At 9:00 p.m. or 10:30 p.m., you are doing nothing but driving. Some dudes would drive up and down the streets hollering at females. Honestly, she will not go with you if you do not own a nice car or have a real great mouthpiece on you. I am talking about the straight game. But it's worth a shot. However, I advise you to just keep it straightforward—like, "Hey, sweetie, how're you doing? I see you are in a hurry. Do us both a favor; input my number in your phone, and hit me when you get settled in the crib." That line might work if you trying to get yourself a date. But no, that's not your objective tonight. I want you to walk straight up to her and just say, "Do you want to drink with me?"

Within the first six seconds, this woman has already decided if she wants to fuck with you or not. Try not to drown her out by continuously asking for her number. Remember, family, she is walking, and her fucking with you should be an honor, unless you are just as broke as her. Now, you have approximately a 60 percent chance she might just hit you up and take your offer, and if you obtain her number during the encounter, remember that women do not usually like to be the first one to call. However, if she does call, the rest is in your hands. Here's another scenario you might encounter during a ride looking for a street thot. If you saw a woman with a "dude" waiting at a bus stop, and he just looks like he's just standing there, it could be her man. You are thinking to yourself, "Damn, if she was not with him, I will shoot my shot." Please stop thinking that way; in this scenario, you need to be clever. You ask her if she is single and if that is her man. Don't be scared to ask, too, because it is compelling and disrespectful but smart in so many ways. Target all your questions toward her, and pay no attention to the gentleman standing next to her. Let me elaborate on this. You just told the dude whom she was standing with or talking to, "You ain't shit, and right now, I have your girl's attention." Secondly, you said to the woman, "I notice you and want you, and the dude you are with doesn't like you." Thirdly, you ask a question that puts him on the defense and puts that woman on the offense. Usually, the conversation would go like, "Hey buddy, is that your girl?" In this case, his response would be, "Yeah." Six out of ten men would lie in this situation. This is their first encounter/first date, or he probably just met her five minutes ago. And this lame is giving her a title already.

When you redirect that question toward the woman, she will usually tell the truth. Her response will be, "Not at all; this is just my friend," or "Yes, this is my man." Believe me, that dude that she is with won't say shit at all because (1) he wants to know how tight his game is, (2) he wants to know what she thinks they are, and (3) he wants to know if she is about to give out her number. If she does give the number, I then know that she ain't shit. Look at it this way; you just helped both of them out. Try that out the next time you are driving. Most likely you will get her number, because you took authority and weren't scared to talk to her in the presence of a guy she is with.

I recall one day when I was getting some gas. I saw this "li'l thotty" walking to the gas station. I was pumping gas on pump 3, and another guy was pumping gas on pump 4. I said, "Shorty right there. Oh, she looks beautiful. He replied, "You are right about that, and I am going to see if I can take her home tonight with me."

I started laughing. He said, "For real, bro, watch this. When she comes out of the gas station, I'm going to make that happen."

I sat there waiting like a dog waiting to be fed, thinking to myself, "What is he about to do?" and "Will it work?" I thought this stranger must be insane, on some drugs or something to think that this woman will go home with him and let him smash on the first night, let alone a strange guy at 11:00 p.m.! He must be trippin'. Just then, he spoke twelve magical words that I will never forget: "Hey, sweetie, how would you like to come home with me tonight?"

She looked at him and said with laughter, "Boy, I don't even know you," with a laugh that could make clouds move. He replied, "But you could tonight."

She laughed and said, "I have to go home and take a shower first." Then, they exchanged numbers. At that point, I realized that I needed ten boxes of Magnums because I was about to go on a fucking spree. I learned two things that night: women want dick just like men want pussy, and the less you try to get sex from a woman, the more willing she will be to have sex with you.

CHAPTER 3

Greyhound Station Thots

The second spot you should be hitting up around 11:30 p.m. to midnight is the bus station. Note: This usually works when the weather is bad. Look, you do not have to go out of your city to fuck different women. I know you are thinking, "Damn, do I need to catch a bus to get a thot from the station?" The answer is "No, sir." You are looking for women who just came into the city and the ones who are layovers. In my opinion, these women are the sleaziest. Think about it: she is stuck in town for a few hours, and she wouldn't want to be cramped up, sleeping on a bench all night. At that precise time, when you come to the bus station, she will ask, "Where are you headed?" or "Did you just miss your bus also?" Your answer should be "Yes, I did." Now she feels like you can relate to her situation. During your conversation, gradually insist that she should turn up with you, meaning you and she should drink until the bus arrives. Now, factor in the time her bus will arrive. As soon as you find out when her bus will arrive, you should insist that you need to go talk to customer service to know when exactly your bus is arriving. With that transpiring, as you head to talk to customer service, turn back around and say to her, "I'm going for a drink, and you should join

me." She is in a thinking process, deciding whether she feels like fucking with you that night or not.

When you come back from speaking to customer service, ask her if she is ready to go get this drink. Now, either she is coming or not. If she says "no," you say "okay." Exchange numbers, and make your exit. More than likely, you should be expecting a call from her later on that night. If she has a layover, she will regret why she didn't fuck with you when she had a chance, unless you came off as a creep or being too thirsty for the pussy. Now, if she says yes to your proposal, then you are in the game. Remember this process of getting a bus thot should only take fifteen to thirty minutes, ten minutes if you found a woman who is coming into the city. Now, if she says yes, you should already have in the trunk of your car. If questions ever comes up such as, "Why do you have a bottle of liquor in your trunk?" and "Why is your car parked here if you're catching the bus?" your response is "I'm always preparing for any situation." Secondly, you should have parked your vehicle in the parking lot, to avoid the second question. What you should be saying also is, "Can I show you the city for a while?" Your approach should be subtle and straightforward—for instance, "Hey, you should get some dick while you are here in the city," without saying, "Hey, do you want some dick before you go back home?"

Now, if she is not trying to fuck with you like that, then that's not the thot you're looking for that night. She does not want to visit your crib and kick it; don't even waste your time playing around with

her. However, you should have already established this before you pull off in your car, and that is just real talk.

14

CHAPTER 4

Club Thots

You should have a motel on standby for this night because you can fuck three different women in that time if you play it right. From now on, whenever you go to the club or a lounge to talk to women, you are from out of town. You do not know the city, and the line for that night is "I'm only here for the night, one or two days." Hypothetically speaking, if you live in Cleveland and you have been there all your life, you know the ins and outs of your city, but you tell that woman you live in Washington DC and that you're visiting family that stays out there. This may sound crazy, but it's not. Because once you say that, in her mind, you just gave her an invitation to have a one-night stand with you.

The next question she would ask is, "Oh, so how often do you come to this city?" Your reply should be short and simple: "Once a year" or "Every three months." Women love out-of-town dick just like men love out-of-town pussy. because there are no strings attached. There's a good chance of her going back to your motel or hotel with you because

(1)you do not live there,

(2) she wants to know how out-of-town dick feels, and

(3) you are not fucking up what she has got going on in her life. What I mean by that is, if she came to the bar/club to blow off some steam because her and her boyfriend/husband just pissed her off, then congratulations: you just became a candidate for her to get fucked that night. She will not worry about bumping into you one day by accident and be in that awkward situation or worry about you calling her constantly because by doing that type of shit, you just might get her caught up with her man.

Now, you might ask yourself, "What if we accidentally run into each other one day after that?" You should just say, "I am here for three months on an urgent business trip," and then you quickly exit, saying you are running late for a meeting and that she should text you later. This prevents her from asking any curious questions that you are not prepared to answer. This gives you time to make up a good story if you choose to talk to her later.

CHAPTER 5

Online Thots (OTs)

Getting a thot from a dating app or a social media site like Pof or Instagram could not be any easier. But today's lesson is getting off your ass so you can get some face-to-face interaction. That being said, Facebook would be the easiest site to accomplish this. You get six to nine notifications of the same women liking something that you post on your timeline. Yup, you guessed right—she wants to fuck you or thinks you are handsome. However, this theory works both ways. I had always thought this was a weak way to get women. If you meet her off the internet, usually there's something fucked up about her. And the real reality is that there's something fucked about you also. Men who rely on dating women solely online rather than going out to meet them have something extremely wrong with them also. A man who does this is lazy. Women like to be persuaded. Instead of finding a woman in a social environment, you chose the easy way out. However, look at it this way: at least now both of you can state all your fucked flaws to each other. The funny thing about these sites is she might not know she is posting thot material on her timeline, or even in her wall status. Women will say, "Damn, I dated some stupid guys." My favorite post a woman might make: "The last guy I was with, wasn't on shit." If she dates nothing-ass dudes constantly, you guessed right; she is a nothing-ass female.

Now, let us get back to the subject at hand. When looking for a social site to catch a thot, you should always first view the picture gallery. The picture that you are looking for usually looks like she is auditioning to be a stripper. Examples would be that she is always taking half-naked pictures, or a picture that has three girlfriends, but all of her friends are under five, and they look pop. This means that one or two of her girlfriends are thots also; it is inconsequential because when they go out, she most likely gets all of the attention. She hangs with them because she is attention greedy. Look at her pictures; this is what you are looking out for. What you are looking for is half-naked pictures of her, and she has two to three ugly friends. Now if she has three girlfriends, two of them are low-key thots also, but they are real discreet with their shit. Hypothetically speaking, if an orgy occurred, the third woman would not participate in that event. The third woman gets excited by what her friends are doing but never would act on those types of encounters. Secondly, reading her posts on her wall is critical and vital information. You will want to look out for a status like "I am bored and horny" or "Who wants to take me out?" or, alternatively, "In need of a cuddle buddy." These types of posts are an invitation indirectly, saying, "Hey, I want to have some fun and get some dick at the end of the night."

Once you see these posts like this, make your approach. But beware: this thot might be trying to get a free meal. Never offer to take her out to eat if you just want to fuck. And if she is on that same agenda as you, pick a day during the week when a restaurant has a food deal like "dollar taco Tuesday."Now, when messaging a thot online, you only have one to two messages to get her attention because you have other fuckboys with the same objective as you. So you have to make the first one count! You don't post your intent on her wall: post that shit in her DM. Send that shit right into her inbox. Don't be like the ten other guys on her page that are sending kiss-face emojis. When you DM her, it becomes personal. If she decides to hang out with you, you should then ask her if she drinks or smokes. If she is a drinker, typically a guy will ask her which drinks she prefers, white or dark liquor. Do not ask her what her favorite or preferred drink is. Because if you, do, you just said, "Hey, I want to buy you your favorite drink." You want her to be fun and tipsy on the way to whatever spot you will be taking her. That decision alone ruins the chances of her asking you to buy her a drink when you get to the destination. If you chose to still get her a drink, you must keep in mind the twenty-dollar budget we discussed earlier. An example would be buying an eleven- or twelve-dollar bottle of alcohol beforehand. And the remaining eight or nine dollars could have been spent on drinks at the bar, and you still have change to tip the bartender or not. Now, if she asks you to buy her a drink while you all are at a spot, and you decided not to, you tell her that you have a bottle in the car and there's no need for that. Say something like, "I could waste money on buying you a drink, or we can go get these tacos after this bar ends." Note that food always overpowers women.

Now, if she doesn't drink or smoke, that means she likes dancing. And the best place to go for that is your house. You're the coldest DJ she will ever hear or meet.

CHAPTER 6

Ratchet Thots (RTs)

Some women have sex with no morals. I mean it does not get any lower than this. These thots are down to fuck you wherever you pull your dick out; she would most likely have sex with you in front of her kid. These types of women are likely to be found at house parties or get-togethers formally known as kickbacks. Now, I'm not saying that every damn woman that goes to a kickback is a thot. What I'm saying is that a thot in there somewhere. Now, on arriving at the scene of the kickback, look for children under the age of five running around the house. Secondly, look for that child's mother. Then, you should observe if she is smoking or drinking. Observe the crowd in the house to determine whether they are "turning up." Check the time. If it is past 7:00 p.m., and that mother still has her child up, apparently, she doesn't care about letting her child be around this type of environment. That means she is the kind of woman that would have sex with you on the same night. You will be in her room giving her that D with her child also in the bedroom. And she would respond, saying that the child won't remember anything because the child is four years old. I hear so many stories about these types of situations, and I came to find out that they are true.

The Ratchet Thot Test

Sometimes you must give the women you want to be with the ratchet thot test; this test is only for a woman if you plan on keeping her around. Say it is the first time you were kicking it with a chick, and you bring her to your house/spot. I want you to leave some money on the bathroom floor or anywhere that you think she would potentially stumble into. Make sure the amount is at least ten to twenty dollars. Only you know where you put this money. Now, after you have both had fun partying like you all just went to Vegas, check and see if your money is still in the same place where you left it. If it is she might not be an RT. However, if the money's gone, she failed the ratchet test. Don't confront her about it, at least not at that moment. Wait till she starts catching feelings and starts asking you question like "When are we going to take things to the next level?" Then you respond to her, saying, "Hell, we cannot, and this is why." Tell her she did not pass the RT test. My father always said if a person will steal from you, then that person will also lie to you.

CHAPTER 7

Hidden Thots

These are my favorite types of thots because it is like playing that game "Where's Waldo?" Instead, it's more like "Let's find a thot." Women hate to admit to anybody that their best friends are thots, maybe because they don't want to be thought of as thots too. Truthfully, 75 percent of the time, a woman is a thot on the low as well. You must listen really close to what this woman is telling you because if she is in a relationship or even married, she gives off signals that say, "Hey, I want some dick, but I am not going to say it out loud."

I remember I was in the lounge dancing with this woman. She told me she was married. I was like "Cool," but I was still about to try and talk to her. She was not attempting to come home with me that night. However, we started having conversations, and she secretly told me some days she has single days. A "single day" means she is single, just single for that day alone. She's not single the next day or the next week. It's a secret day that she feels she needs to be free. She said that "she only becomes single like that when she comes out to bars/clubs and dances"; that shit did not make any sense to my guy that overheard it, but to me, I understood that code. It means music turns

her on, and it is sort kind of therapy for her. It also meant, "I want you to come dance with me later on this week."

Your pitch to a situation like this is two ways. Say to her, "Come, help me make up this new dance I am trying to create," or say, "Let's go dancing." It's okay if you don't know how to dance, but with enough drinks in your system and in hers, I'm pretty sure you will be moonwalking across the dance floor. Now ask her, "Do you want to come out with me again and dance?" She most likely will say yes. When she says yes, say, "Can you come to my house to make up a dance after we hit the bar?" But when she gets your place, you'd better to have music and alcohol ready. Now the rest is history.

Equally important, women who claim they do not have any female friends and that they only hang around males are hidden thots also. These are the voluminous thot and liars. There is a seven out of ten possibility they are fucking the whole squad. She always claims she does not get along with females. That is because she keep fucking her man friends, of course. Women are easy to understand if you listen to them; I stress this firmly. First, you must understand about this thot that she wants you to treat her like one of your guys. However, I do not mean talking to her about fucking other chicks; that subject only works if this thot is into women. You should be steered away from that subject until you have hit it at least twice. Then you could say, "My female friend thought you were cute," and her response might be "Let me see her pic." If she looks attractive enough to her, then you both will hit it. For you to have sex with this type of thot, all you have to do is take her to places you and your guys go, such as bars or gamerooms. Believe it or not, there are many women who will like to do thing like this. Keep in mind there's no need to sugarcoat that you want to have sex with her that night. While both of you are having a real time, gradually say, "You're not getting any dick tonight." It is blunt but effective. It's effective because she has no leverage over you anymore.

Here's a quick lesson about two different types of women. With a real woman who has her shit together, her pussy is like winning the lottery: everybody wants to hit it. A thot pussy is like a slot machine: if you can't hit it on a couple tries, move on to the next machine. Every woman knows while she is on a date with a guy or even talking on the phone whether she is coming to his house or not. Women have already decided this before you establish that you want to have sex with her. They know whether they were or not going to give you some pussy that night. I always found it intriguing for women to say, "Hey, I am not having sex with you on the first night." This is so classic for women to say. However, there are ways around that. If you have plans to meet up with a chick that day, make your date at 7:00 p.m. Now, I want you to have activities set up for her and you to do all the way up until 1:00 a.m. Now, if you play it right, you should come off having sex that night. You should know your city and what's going on that night. Moreover, if you do not, then there's always Eventbrite and Groupon, but remember, find something to do that will keep you in that budget we discussed earlier. Now, when the clock hits 1:00 a.m., you and she should both be liquored up. You see when the clock runs around midnight, it is the next day. By this time, she has spent two days with you. If you were keeping her interested the whole day, you should be good to go. However, if you did not smash, which is kind of rare, most likely you will get it sometime next week.

Retired Hidden Thot

I am going to keep this short and straight to the point. Have you ever had this conversation with a woman? She says, "I am not having sex with men until I get married," but you come to find out she has a kid. This is a bright-red flag right away. She is lying; don't believe that shit. What she is saying to you is, "Hey, I fucked too many dudes in my past, and I am trying to see if I could run this BS on you." Chances are she had sex last week. If she claims to be abstinent from sex, she is lying, because she is getting off some way. The thots are between the ages of twenty-eight and thirty-six who usually claim this fuckery. Most of them want you to court them. If she tries hitting you with the scheme of "I'm not having sex with you for ninety days," walk away. It's just that simple. Don't even waste your time and money on her.

CHAPTER 8

Job Thots—Be Careful!

If you love your job, don't try to fuck anyone there. This is for the ones who don't give a fuck about their jobs. I want to touch base on this subject briefly. Most likely you have some high-maintenance thots who have jobs like working for McDonalds or Walmart; they are CNAs or have home-care jobs. These are just a few places where a variety of thots might be working. These types of women act like they work for the government and are getting paid twenty-two dollars an hour when, in reality, they are on minimum wage. Don't let this thot bamboozle you. She has probably fucked everybody in the workplace. No matter what job you are working, there are always going to be thots in there somewhere. Remember, the most valuable person in every company is the custodian or security guard. These people know everything about everyone. To get this thot, you must become more than just her coworker. You must become the coworker; you must present yourself as a boss at all times, a boss outside your workplace. Don't be running around your job like a minimanager. You must be that go-to guy when there's a new party or new event going on. Bring that information back to work that Monday; brag about how "turnt up" this place was, and mention, "You should have been there." Do this for three weeks straight. And

in the fourth week, invite her out; most importantly, invite her out on payday. The reason is that you know she can buy her own drinks. Keep in mind that you're still sticking to that budget that we talked about earlier, and the same rules apply to her ass too.

CHAPTER 9

What Is a Fuckboy?

This chapter of the book will cover male thots, formerly known as fuckboys. Fuckboys are not always easy to spot in the wild, given their highly adaptive nature and ability to blend in. Any bitch who's been through the Amazon jungle of dating knows that meeting a fuckboy now is like finding a Rattata in the original Gameboy Pokémon—it's common AF, but you always know it is something better. The key to getting a fuckboy in your life is to know how to identify early signs of fuckboyism. Here are some telltale signs the guy you're dating is a fuckboy.

Fuckboy, which can be stylized as "fuccboi," "fucboi," or a permutation thereof, has been creeping into the English language in the last few years, most notably online. In fact, Google deciphers that people have been using the term "fuckboy" and searching for its definition increasingly since around April 2013 onward.

But what is a fuckboy? Where has it come from, and what the fuck does it mean? The issue with the word fuckboy is that it's immature—I don't mean necessarily in use, but because it is still in the early stages of its development. Due to its immaturity, fuckboy is a linguistic black hole. Its origin is most likely in prison slang, where it is said to refer to men who are "gay for pay." Other sources directly connect

the term to prison rape. Fuckboy has also been associated with gay male culture when referring to men who take submissive roles during sex.

But the online etymology of fuckboy was changed by internet trolls. The term was adopted on anonymous online platforms typically used for slut-shaming and suicide encouragement. So the word's genesis isn't the most pleasant of tales, but surely no swear word's is. Shit comes from shit after all. Due to the word being associated with rap and prison slang, fuckboy was cited as having misogynistic and homophobic overtones. For example, in 2004, the Urban Dictionary listed its first description of a fuckboy as "a person who is a weak ass pussy that ain't about shit." This sort of curse is nothing new or impressive. But, in the second entry, written a decade later in 2014, fuckboys are described differently and in much greater detail. There is a list of particular traits, such as "relies on his mom but doesn't respect women" and "can't find the clitoris."

The Online Slang Dictionary perhaps had the most recent and concise definition of the word on the internet: "fuck boy: woman oppressor." When describing how smartphone apps have intensified the dynamics of hookup culture in the last decade, a fuckboy lives on social media looking for easy women or thots to fuck. A fuckboy is a young man who sleeps with women without any intention of having a relationship with them or perhaps even walking them to the door postsex. He's a womanizer, an especially callous one, as well as kind of a loser.

One thing is clear—the word fuckboy seems to have come to specifically refer to a man who is self-absorbed as well as emotionlessly and carelessly sexually promiscuous. It could be argued that we could call these sexually promiscuous man "man whores" or "male sluts," but the necessity of those masculine modifiers drives home the fact that whores and sluts are inherently female. Furthermore, words such as these refer to someone's presumed number of sexual partners, whereas "fuckboy" incorporates a direct attack on the person's character.

Fuckboy is therefore significant in part simply because it's new. It is filling a gap in our current language of labels. When it comes to labels, there is a renowned gendered imbalance. Consider the contrast between "slut"or "slag" with "player" or "stud" or between "spinster" and "bachelor." Women are particularly at risk of being pigeonholed or packed up into small, stereotypical, derogatory boxes. They can be verbally attacked for their looks, sexual history, intellect, and moral code. Swear words aimed at men, although offensive, are less descriptive and usually equate to them being unpleasant people. In fact, the harshest words aimed at men are ones that either accuse them of being homosexual or effeminate or refer directly to female genitalia. Calling a horrible specimen of an man a "dickhead" doesn't quite govern the same authority as calling him a "cunt." That much is true. But why is it that when referring to loathsome, odious people, the harshest insults out there are dependent on negatively referring to women's bodies? These words become misogynistic by default because they inexorably insult women in the process.

Fuckboy is plugging this gender gap in swearing. It can be used by men and women alike with the same amount of gusto. Also, significantly, there is no female equivalent. Fuckboys have always existed in some form or another, but previously their behavior wasn't pointed out as wrong. Arguably, the word has come to stand for those who find it most contemptible in a man. But the word represents progression because it signifies a shift in society that recognizes and points out a male culture that is no longer considered standard or appropriate in modern living. There will always be jerks/assholes out there. Just make sure you not dealing with a fuckboy.

CHAPTER 10

How To Spot A Fuckboy (Guest Writer)

When I first heard the term "fuckboy," I thought it was a little harsh. I mean, I get that some guys can be players, some can be assholes, and some can be selfish (all one and the same, really), but "fuckboy"—I mean, wow! Then I thought about what women are called: "slut," "skank," "whore," or my favorite, "thot," and I came to the realization that these so-called "gentlemen" needed at least one name to settle the score. Enter the appreciation of "fuckboy."

What is a fuckboy? Let's start by breaking this word down. The word "fuck" is an English word, an obscene word which refers to the act of sexual intercourse and is also commonly used to denote disdain of a person, and a "boy" is a male child, not a man. So a "fuckboy" is an obscenely behaved male child. On Urban Dictionary, the definitions are sparse and somewhat frightening. They range from "a manipulating dick who does whatever it takes to benefit him, regardless of whom he screws over," to "the lowest possible form of the vile, degenerate waste pouring from the proverbial asshole of society." According to Pacific Standard, "a fuckboy is not a dating style [or necessarily single guy] as much as a worldview that reeks of entitlement but is aghast at the prospect of putting in an effort."

Ultimately, a "fuckboy" is a guy who doesn't respect women. At their worst they are narcissistic tools who refer to women by previously mentioned unflattering terms. At their best they are guys who make you feel like you owe them something you can't quite put your finger on, while insisting to others you aren't exclusive. We have all been there. Anyway, I digress. The main thing you need to hear: stay the fuck away from the "fuckboy". Here is how to spot one of these assholes from afar!

He Is Forward

At the beginning, this right-looking charmer is forward, insistent, and irresistible. As you get further down the road, you will realize that he behaves this way with every girl he meets. But when you voice displeasure with sad behavior, after he has made you feel a little crazy, he will tell you exactly what you want to hear: "You are overthinking it. I would never want anyone but you." Oh, he will!

He Is Obsessed with Social Media

This guy is all about his image. He untags photos on Facebook that feature you or any girl in particular. On Instagram, he follows a bunch of Insta-models and likes all their photos, just in case. On Snapchat, he requests you download immediately upon meeting and proceeds to make you feel like you owe him sexy pictures. To top it all off, if you go anywhere near his phone, you are out—and deep down you know why.

He Puts In Very Little Effort

First, if he doesn't blow you off, he only wants to go out with you during the workweek—weekends are a no-go. Second, he always texts and never calls you, expecting you to be the one who constantly follows up. Third, he never shows you affection in public unless no one is around, and finally, he booty calls you late at night. The sneaky way a fuckboy booty calls, though, is to make you feel as you are in a relationship with him, so the booty call is your choice too.

He Can't Define What You Are

When you are dating a real fuckboy, you always feel as you are on the cusp of the talk, but months go by and you are nowhere near being his girlfriend. Although you have no idea about some women in his life, when you finally do bring up enough courage to talk relationship after desperately hoping you won't scare him off, he reveals that he "doesn't believe in labels." You deserve better!

His Friends Are the Same

A group of great-looking charmers who are all "best mates" and treat girls like shit? Run.

Beware of the Nice Fuckboy

It's not easy to keep up with the extensive personalities of guys you should steer clear from while navigating the hookup generation. We have so many variations of the good guy and the bad guy, but what is even more confusing is when the guy is a mixture of the two.

He acts like a good guy, and perhaps deep down he is. He believes he is up front and to the point, but he simultaneously plays games, with sex being his primary motivation.

He's all about his friends, and the girl he is talking to or hooking up with comes last. He can easily be switched out for a number of different girls. When he's with you, he acts like a genuinely nice guy and wants your company. But when you part ways, that's it for him.

If you see each other or happen to run into each other, you'd interact or maybe go home with each other, but other than that, there isn't much of a effort. It's frustrating because when you are with this person, it can feel good while inadvertently sparking a sense of hope. He isn't a jerk, and he isn't rude. He doesn't promise you things or set any expectations. At the same time, he makes you feel happy, only to ignite expectations that can never be met.

The nice fuckboy can make you feel great when you are with him, leaving you disappointed when apart. He can tell you he's not looking for anything serious or make it clear it is just a sexual relationship and nothing past that. Without being formally rejected, you can feel heavily rejected. Even though he isn't choosing you, this doesn't make him a lousy person. He may act like a fuckboy for a number of reasons that are just out of your control. But that's his problem.

Maybe he has commitment issues. Maybe he had a shitty past experience. Maybe he has trust issues. Maybe there is something going on with him that has nothing to do with you, and for that reason, it's not your place to try and force your way through.

Even if he isn't intentionally trying to hurt you, he is still cutting you. Don't ignore this reality. The fact that he is hurting you, intentionally or not, it is what you need to accept. You may feel like you can help him, change him, or even save him. Guys will almost always have sex with you. If a guy believes he's done everything to make you aware that he isn't looking for anything serious, he may feel like he has done everything he needed to do on his end, avoiding any guilt for any attachment you may gain. As hard as it may be to let go, you have to.

This is not a fulfilling relationship. You are setting yourself up for disappointment each time you talk to or spend time with the nice fuckboy. Holding on inevitably will block you from new potential relationships. He may be a nice guy. But he's not your nice guy. Stop wasting your time with the nice fuckboy. He's not for you. There is a nice guy out there for you who will undoubtedly choose you from the start.

CHAPTER 11

On Fuckboys and How to Avoid Them

You've spent days staring at your phone wondering why it's been two weeks, and you still haven't received a text back from the guy you're dating. You go over every detail of your relationship in your head trying to figure out what you've done wrong. This is what you've done wrong: you decided to date a fuckboy! Spotting a fuckboy is easy when you know what one actually is. Just look for all of the things that make him a fuckboy, and you'll know that you've found one. Lucky you. Here are some giveaway signs that a guy you may know or know of is a fuckboy, so you won't feel like a complete ass.

They have no remorse for what they're doing to the girls they're playing. When you view the situation from the outside looking in, it seems like the fuckboy actually has no feelings at all, even if he tells a girl (or multiple girls) that he loves them.

He knows exactly how to get into your head or your friend's head. If you want to spot a fuckboy in a guy that someone you know is involved with, he does it without his victim realizing it. He can control and manipulate a girl without the girl knowing that it's happening. He thinks he can drop you and then pick you up whenever he pleases, and he does this. Sometimes he'll just stop talking to you because

he's bored or something, and you're left wondering what you've done wrong, which is another way that a fuckboy can get in your head. He can flip things on you and make you think that it's you who's done something wrong when it's not you at all, until he suddenly talks to you again a few days or weeks later.

One foolproof way of how to spot a fuckboy is to find out your friends' opinions of the guy. This is so important! Your friends always want what's best for you. Can you hear the screams of frustration coming from me here since I've been that friend way too many times? If your friends don't like him or have "off" feelings toward him, he's bad news. He's a fuckboy. Be done with him.

They enjoy the chase. Fuckboys enjoy the challenge of girls who aren't easy to please. They'll carry on with the chase because when they finally "accomplish their missions," which are definitely the ways they see these girls, it'll make their egos even bigger, and they'll feel fulfilled. Also, once they've finally gotten what they wanted from the girls who are their challenges, they'll be done with them because there's no more excitement in it for them.

They always lead on more than one girl at a time. They'll have the many desperate girls who fall at their feet, despite them being ugly and having the personality of a brick wall in some cases. They'll have the one girl who is a challenge for them. They'll play all of these girls against each other, and then they'll just talk shit about every girl behind her back anyway. They'll say that they have the girls "whipped' and brag about it. Girl, you ain't shit to a fuckboy. You're just another notch on the bedpost for them. I'm sorry I had to use tough love at some point.

They're always changing their minds, and they don't care at all. This links in with them playing many girls at one time because this is the reason they always change their minds about what they want from each girl and who they prefer. This also links in with them having no remorse (the main sociopathic tendency) because they genuinely don't care and don't see any wrong in what they're doing at all.

They're cheaters. If you're the girl who he is flirting with while he has a girlfriend then get out now because if he cheats on someone else to get you, he'll cheat on you to get someone else. I recite it all the time.

So now that you've identified and spotted fuckboys, how are you supposed to avoid them? What do you do if you're already stuck under a spell? What do you do if you see these things happening to some of your friends (these girls, I'm so with you) and want to help? What do you do if a fuckboy has already used you to get what he wanted all along? Let's go through some tips.

If you want to avoid a fuckboy, you'll need to block him out of your life completely. This also goes for what you should do when he's already got what he wanted out of you, because once he's done that, you should just drop him and avoid him. This means blocking him from every form of social media ever (even the ones like Facebook you'd forget, like Ask.fm, WhatAapp, and Tumblr) and blocking his number from texting, calling, or FaceTiming you. Also, ignore him whenever you encounter him in person. Act like he doesn't exist; look straight through him, and do not interact with him. If you're stuck under his spell, but you're now seeing the light; get the fuck outta there. Tell him that you're done with him, and then never speak to him again. Trust me, when you tell him that you're done, you'll feel so satisfied. And let's be real: the fuckboy was just going to drop you like that eventually anyway, so do it to him before he can do it to you. Then just ignore him. Unfollow or unfriend him, and if he ever texts or calls, don't answer. If you ever see him out and about, ignore him. Blocking like I suggested above is optional.

If you are that girl (holla at me) who has to watch as multiple people you know are falling under the spells of fuckboys, then listen up. Do not constantly tell your friend that the guy is bad news! You will push her further away from you and closer to the fuckboy. That's bad news because if you do that, he can easily manipulate her and turn her against you. Give your friend tough love, but don't belittle her. Don't patronize or be repetitive. Say what you feel, but let her have space to make her own judgment. And if your friend does get burned, just be there. No "I told you so." I guarantee you that a few months down the line, you'll all be laughing about how she ever gave a fuckboy the time of day in the first place.

If you've been used by a fuckboy so he could get what he wanted, then be the bigger person; rise above it, and ignore him. Plus, even if you don't say anything, your friends will, so you don't even need to say anything. Let your friends make themselves look bad because they'll be happy to do it if it means they can call out the fuckboy. Think about it this way. You would still be stuck under his spell if you never realized that he was just trying to get what he wanted out of you, so it happened for the best. So rise above it. Oh, and do the thing where you block him out of your life too.

42

CHAPTER 12

Fuckboy Rules

In this chapter, I'll be talking about some rules most fuckboys in town follow to nail pretty girls. But to a fuckboy who is new in the game, first, you should get a haircut with both sides of your head shaved but leave the top. Here you can incorporate a man bun if you so wish. Douse yourself in expensive cologne, roll up your skintight chinos, sleeves, and durries because you're just so much more authentic, and don your best pair of Ray-Bans. Make sure you wear shoes with no socks because socks are lame. Now you're ready to go outside in public. That's just a brief digression anyway. Now let's take a look at some rules these guys follow.

Perfect messaging style. When it comes to messaging like a fuckboy, less is definitely more. Mostly they keep it on Facebook, because they feel having someone's actual number is just too much commitment. Short messages and affiliation with the emoji keyboard. They curate a go-to booty message because no one actually calls these days: "wyd" is always a good one that gets the point across. When they are in doubt of what to say or when they're way too plastered to spell, sending the emoji combo peach-eggplant-squirt gets straight to their mind, displaying their no-fuss attitudes. It's all about time efficiency.

Do drink and pick up. The golden rule of "nothing good happens after 2:00 a.m." has been disproved by the fuckboy, who makes his best pulls in the wee hours of the morning when he has consumed a large amount of alcohol. Fuckboy ensures that when it's time to leave the club, he sends drunk messages to any potential hookups he met that night, and if there is no one new available, he drunkenly contacts all past encounters. Fuckboys always use being drunk as an excuse for everything he does. Sending an apology message the following morning is always a nice touch for him. He is a gentleman after all.

Request nudes. The fuckboy code about this is that "you need to browse before you buy." Can you just imagine?

YTB. Did you know that if there's anything better than one fuckboy, it's a group of fuckboys? Strength in numbers is a valid lesson, and your groups of boys/girls are excellent to help guard them from awkward situations with the opposite sex—for example, when all the people he's banging turn up at the club. He immediately melt into his crowd for protection and to avoid conversing with someone he's dogging/has previously dogged; he uses the excuse of "I'll be back soon; I'm just checking on so-and-so." Situation successfully avoided. Instagram and Snapchat need to be your favorite apps. A fuckboy will use these to keep his options open and make his game even stronger than it already must be. Get your hookup for the night on there, and then hit up her roommate the next day. That's always their impression.

Pretends he wants more when he doesn't. Confusion is the key to the fuckboy lifestyle; he feels the more confused he makes her, the more she'll want him—it's simple. He makes her think he wants more by inviting her over during the day or telling his friends about her because it's the little things that they'll pick up on.

Only hit up someone you're interested in on the weekends. Don't even think about hitting a girl up throughout the week. That is against the fuckboy code 100 percent. The fuckboy lifestyle exists Monday through Sunday, but any talk Monday through Thursday is a direct route to commitment.

Everything happens on his terms. He will never do anything just because she wants to; his happiness (and impressing other fuckboys) is the key to success. He will ask for nudes, but he won't send any. He mostly won't stay at your place just because it's more convenient for you. He will tell you he doesn't want to be exclusive but gets annoyed when you talk to another guy. It's on his terms here.

Sex is the goal. For a fuckboy, sex is the goal, and it needs to be handled properly. That means no emotions or romance. It's just sex. He fist bumps after to congratulate you on a job well done.

CHAPTER 13

Types of Fuckboy

We have all been there: met a guy we liked, whether that be online or in person, and realized that he was not as "nice" as he was made out to be. Whether it is because he is hiding an extra girlfriend (or two) or just using you for sex, this fuckboy knows how to trick you into being his side chick, and trust me, it's not an easy situation to get yourself out of. Let's take a look at some of these fuckboys.

The wannabe player fuckboy. Oh, this fuckboy is so sad. He dresses in a way he thinks is hot and sexy and mature, but you just wonder if he's gay. He frequently buys rounds of drinks for everyone, like for every friend you have. He basically has his shit together; he's a decent guy. He goes out so often that you think he must be scoring, right? Ohm no! He's just a wannabe player. Something about his game does not add up. He probably sucks in bed anyhow.

The Peter Pan fuckboy. He may want you to be his mommy; he may be stuck in high school, he may not. The Peter Pan fuckboy is often camouflaged among the regular bros at the bar. But sooner or later, you'll get the sense that he really has no desire to be an adult. He'll get his career together, he'll get his finances together, he'll finish his MBA, whatever. And you'll think, "Okay, he looks like an adult and smells like

an adult, so why is he still chasing twenty-two-year-old randos at the gym? Why can he not take me on a real date? Why can't he see a good thing when it's right in front of him?" Oh! Probably because he will always be a child. No amount of expensive cologne or a base-model Infiniti will change that.

The "Will you be my mommy?" fuckboy. If you're anything like me, you'll relish taking care of someone. I legitimately enjoy cooking, cleaning, doing laundry, and all that stupid domestic shit. Let me tell you, it does me no good. I often find the "Will you be my mommy?" fuckboy. From the outside, he'll look like a man. He'll have the car, the job, the apartment, whatever. He's got the trappings of adult life. But when it comes down to it, this man needs you to take care of him. And he will never be able to take care of you.

The mindfucker fuckboy. Oh, girl. If you find this one, run the opposite direction. Buy a one-way ticket to Zimbabwe. Anywhere there's no cellphone reception, actually. The kicker about this fuckboy is that you never even really liked him that much. But he will make you think that you're so lucky to be with him. You'll feel constantly anxious, waiting for that following text or phone call. You'll wonder, at random moments, if he knows anything about you at all. Does he give two shits about your dreams? At other minutes, you will feel like you're Kate Winslet in Titanic before the whole Leo-on-the-life-raft buzzkill. Girl, don't. Push him off the life raft. Save yourself!

The user fuckboy. We've all dated this one, unfortunately. Using comes in many shades. There's the fuckboy who financially uses you—he is often a server or bartender, maybe he's in graduate school indefinitely, whatever. There's the fuckboy who emotionally uses you—he has a messed-up family; he will always kinda be in love with his ex. He's tortured by…something. You will pay the price for it. Probably for years, as you try to save him. There's the fuckboy who sexually uses you—I don't have to explain that one, I hope. But here's a tip: he probably only wants to see you at night. You have sex every time you're together, you feel pressured to sexually perform, you feel totally insecure about your appearance. Ring a bell? You know it does.

The delusional fuckboy. Again, this fuckboy can wear many disguises. Perhaps he's delusional about himself. He thinks his dick is huge; he thinks his fashion sense is on fleek. He thinks he's a 10 when he's maybe a 6.5 on a great day when you're drunk and not paying attention. He'll send you gym selfies that are mediocre at best. He thinks he's a sex god. He doesn't understand why he's single; he doesn't understand why he hasn't gotten a promotion. It must be because his boss is a moron, right? Nope. The delusional fuckboy just doesn't get it. Anything. He will continue to run through life, bumping into women and confusing them with his inflated self-worth. I can't tell you how many times I've met this fuckboy and merely walked away, shaking my head. How has he gotten this far in life? We shall never know.

The "never-enough" fuckboy. Ugh. Ugh, ugh, ugh. This is the fuckboy who gets under your skin. Your relationship will actually be good. It'll be satisfying. You'll love him. You'll know he loves you. You'll know! But only like 99 percent. That 1 percent will eat away at you. He will always believe there will be someone better. Heidi Klum could be a legit NASA employee, and he would still think there was a Kate Upton who invented Fruit Roll-Ups and would let him eat them off her huge tits. You'll never be good enough, sweetheart. Strangely, he'll end up with someone average. Not a Kate Upton. Not a Heidi. Not even an Instagram model who used too many filters.

The "never-enough" fuckboy, part II. It's worth noting a distinctive iteration of the never- enough fuckboy. This guy never actually dates or commits to anyone. He'll go on a lot of dates, maybe a maxium of three girls. Again, a woman could be phenomenal, but he'll always find some random reason that he's not ready or that she's not the one. And as his friends date and marry, he'll judge the hell out of them. He'll talk about them settling or make fun of them actually caring about their significant others. But really, he's terrified of anything real. He will probably be alone forever. It'll be sad.

The "I know better" fuckboy. This fuckboy is also known as the mansplaining fuckboy, but I like to think that the "I know better" fuckboy is just a little more condescending and a little more convinced that he's actually superior. At first, you may find his confidence and knowledge about the world exciting. Eventually, you'll realize that he actually doesn't know shit, but not before he's gotten into your head and made you feel like you're a clueless little girl who needs him. This fuckboy will say things like, "You know, there was this article in the Washington Post that..." or "in Lacan's Ethics of Psychoanalysis..." or "the Latin root of that is actually..." Shit. Wait a minute. I totally say all of those things. Am I a fuckboy?

CHAPTER 14

Fuckboy Experience (Guest Writer)

I have had times where I have been able to spot them soon enough, before I fell for their sweet, smooth words. However, I knew this one guy for years, and I became a victim of his fuckboy tendencies. I met this guy around a month ago. We both go to the same university, and I had seen him around before actually getting to meet him. From the first time I saw him, it was a "damn, boy" moment. In terms of looks, he was definitely my type. That being, said I am not one to chase, so I didn't make any sort of move.

Long story short, after some not-so-subtle interference by my friend, we ended up talking and hitting it off right away. Granted, we were drunk; drunk people are typically friendly people. We ended up hanging out in a group that whole night, and by the next morning, he had asked a mutual friend for my number. I was excited, but there was some lousy news. This mutual friend warned that he had a girlfriend back home, and though he didn't show much evidence of this, they had been together for a decently long time. Later that night, he called me, and I've really forgotten that words he said, but I can tell they were some of those sweet words you will hear from a fuckboy who just wants nothing but sex from you. My stupid self never saw that coming because I was getting into him already. Anyway, Peter was a terrific friend last year and we were like the chillest friends ever. That's before we started to talk. So we went on a date around Thanksgiving break, and then we hung out during Christmas break. He tried to have sex with me, and I didn't let him. He got into his little petty mood, and I brought this guy back to my halls, and when we got there, he kept asking if he should get a condom from the desk, despite my repeated assurances that a condom would not be necessary as we were not going to have sex. He had a hard time believing this (because who would dare turn down such a fine specimen?), but it was okay. When we got back to my room, things got really weird. He asked me if I had ever heard of a song called "Danzon" (I had not). Then, he played it while making out with me and stroking my back in time to the song. I could tell he was good at this, and I got cought off guard. He started making some moves, and I didn't know when I let go, so I was like okay, and then I decide to lose my virginity to this guy for some reason. Oh! I won't forget that moment. To be honest, I regret it so much.

Although we got along for some time, anyway, I was not really feeling it because he started coming up with some unusual attitude. I could remember there was a day I had to take lunch an hour early to cover for my sick boss that night. One of us had to be there at all times. I opened the front door, and I met him with another lady on the couch, clothes scattered on the floor, scurrying to cover up. It's burned into my head. At that point, it gets blurry. I froze for a second. I started seeing red and knew that if I didn't get out of there, something bad would happen, so I left. I got in my car, locked the door, turned off my cell phone, and started driving. I went back to work and pretended nothing happened. Since then, I stopped calling, and he did the same. We both went different ways and stopped seeing each other. I still feel he cheated on me, though, but anytime I think about that, I'll just decide that was his main motive, and he never meant well for me in the first place. There are more stories about Peter, but I'll just stop here.

If a person wants to talk to you, he will talk to you. It sounds simple, but I think we forget this more than we like to admit. He won't insult your intelligence by giving lame excuses, like he was "too busy" or he "had a long day and didn't have the time to text you." That's complete and utter bullshit. I've said it before, and I'll say it until I die: no one in this whole world is too busy to send a text message. I've sent texts while at work, in class, in the shower, while presenting, in my sleep, while on a plane—anywhere and everywhere. Tell that fuckboy to miss you with the drama. I'm speaking in general now when I say that you don't want a fuckboy to get in your head and control you so much that you end up doing something severe that you didn't actually want to do, or so much that you end up feeling like a mug who's had her heart broken. Girls deserve way better than that. And if all else fails, play him at his own game (I'm joking; don't do that because then it makes you just as low as him, but it's a fun form of revenge if you're the friend of someone who encountered a fuckboy *evil laugh*). Just remember that karma is a beautiful thing. The fuckboy will probably end up losing his job or failing his exams or something because he spent too much time playing multiple girls instead of focusing on bettering his life and career.

53

CHAPTER 15

Conclusion

All things considered, you were trying to buy sex or love, when really you should have analyzed your approach to dating. Understanding thots or fuckboys only takes looking at them as a whole. You have been standing too close to the picture, being mesmerized by a mirage. But once you stand back from it, then and only then can you recognize it as its true imagery. Never treat a thot like she going to be your wife, and, ladies, never cater to a fuckboy's ego.

9 780692 076811